GIRLZ
Netball
Showdown

Jacqueline Arena

illustrated by
Lloyd Foye

MACMILLAN

First published in 2005 by
MACMILLAN EDUCATION AUSTRALIA PTY LTD
15–19 Claremont Street, South Yarra 3141
Reprinted 2005, 2007, 2011, 2012 (twice)

Visit our website at www.macmillan.com.au or
go directly to www.macmillanlibrary.com.au

Associated companies and representatives throughout the world.

Copyright © Jacqueline Arena 2005

All rights reserved.
Except under the conditions described in the *Copyright Act 1968* of Australia
and subsequent amendments, no part of this publication may be reproduced,
stored in a retrieval system, or transmitted in any form or by any means,
electronic, mechanical, photocopying, recording or otherwise, without the
prior written permission of the copyright owner.

National Library of Australia
Cataloguing-in-Publication data

Arena, Jacqueline.

Netball showdown.

For primary school students.
ISBN 978 0 7329 9884 4.
ISBN 978 0 7329 9876 9 (Set 1).
ISBN 0 7329 9884 0.
ISBN 0 7329 9876 X (Set 1).

1. Netball – Juvenile fiction. I. Title. (Series:
Girlz rock!).

A823.4

Series created by Felice Arena and Phil Kettle
Project Management by Limelight Press Pty Ltd
Cover and text design by Lore Foye
Illustrations by Lloyd Foye

Printed in China

GIRLZ ROCK!

Contents

Rachel   *Ellie*

CHAPTER 1

Cut Out for Netball?

Best friends Ellie and Rachel are
trying out Ellie's new netball at their
local netball court.

Rachel "This ball's so good. It feels
really nice. You must be stoked
that your mum bought it for you."

Rachel aims for the netball ring
and shoots. It's a perfect shot. The
ball drops right through the ring and
falls to the ground.

Ellie "Yeah, I s'pose so. She thought
I might like to get into it more—
netball I mean. Y'know, play in a
team or something, like you do."

Rachel "Great idea! You should come to training with me sometime."

Ellie "As if. Aren't you forgetting that I'm hopeless at most sports?"

Rachel "Oh yeah. I remember when you had a go at tennis. You threw your racquet into the air and nearly knocked out some pigeons!"

Both girls giggle.

Rachel has another shot at the ring and shoots another goal.

Rachel "Maybe you just haven't found a sport that suits you. I wouldn't give up yet. Netball just might end up being your thing."

Ellie "D'you think?"

Rachel "Y'never know till you give it a go. Here, have a shot."

Rachel hands the ball to Ellie.

Rachel "C'mon. You can do it. Ready? Shoot!"

CHAPTER 2

Ball Robbers

Ellie aims, then throws the netball up towards the ring. It's such an awful shot that the ball whizzes past the ring and over the fence that surrounds the court.

Ellie "See, I'm terrible."

Rachel "No, you're not. It's only your first shot. You just didn't realise how strong you are."

While the girls talk, the ball is gaining speed as it rolls down the hill.

Rachel "Hey, the ball!"

Ellie "Hurry, before it hits the soccer field and those two guys!"

The two girls chase after the ball. It lands on the soccer field at the bottom of the hill.

Ellie "Hey! What are those guys doing? They're stealing my netball."

Rachel "They better not be!"

Rachel sprints towards the boys. Ellie, who is feeling a bit nervous, waits for a moment then follows. By the time Ellie catches up with Rachel the boys have raced off with the ball in the direction of the netball court.

Ellie "What did you say to them? How come they still have my ball?"

Rachel "I said I'd challenge them to a netball shoot-out to get the ball back. They laughed but said okay. Now, there's a catch …"

Ellie "I don't like the sound of this."

Rachel "We all have to take two shots each. The team with the most goals wins the ball. It's gonna be a netball showdown!"

Ellie "You're not meaning me too, are you? Why me? I'm terrible. That's why we're in this mess. You can take my shots for me."

Rachel "But we both have to shoot—
it's that or nothing. We can beat
these wimpy guys. Boys can't play
netball anyway."

Ellie "I hope you're right."

The girls head back to the netball
court where the two boys are waiting
with Ellie's ball.

CHAPTER 3

Bulldog Boy and Snail Boy

The boys choose Ellie to go first in
the netball showdown. Ellie throws
her two shots. As predicted, she
misses both times.

Ellie "Sorry Rach."

Rachel "Don't worry yet. Let me sink my two in and hopefully they'll miss their shots."

As Rachel prepares to take her first shot at goal, the boys try to put her off by putting their fingers inside their mouths and making popping noises.

Rachel "If you guys don't shut it, I'm gonna …"

Ellie "Ignore them, Rach. Don't get them mad. Look how big they are."

Rachel (whispering) "Yeah! They look like two big baboons. Actually, the smaller one looks like a bulldog with his little pug nose and droopy eyes. He's Bulldog Boy!"

Ellie "Yeah, and did you see how
slowly the other one runs?"
Ellie and Rachel "Yep, he can be
Snail Boy from now on!"

Rachel takes her shot and the ball
swishes through the ring.

Ellie (excitedly) "Yes! How's that,
  Snail Boy and ... oops! I mean ..."

The boys sneer at the girls.

Rachel "She said 'make it sail, boy'.
  She sometimes calls me 'boy'."

Rachel takes her second shot.
Again, she gets it in.

Rachel "Yes! That's two for the girls. Now it's your turn, losers."

Rachel winks at Ellie as she tosses the ball to the boys. Snail Boy takes his shots. He misses the first but gets his second throw in. Then it's Bulldog Boy's first turn. He also gets a goal.

Rachel "It's two goals all. If he gets this one ..."

Ellie "If he gets this one, it's goodbye to my new ball forever! Miss, miss, please miss."

Bulldog Boy throws the netball high into the air. It floats for several seconds before dropping directly through the middle of the ring. The boys win.

Ellie "I don't believe it! Mum's gonna kill me! We've gotta get my ball back."

Rachel "Don't worry, I've got another idea."

CHAPTER 4

It's Not Over Yet

The boys race off with Ellie's new
netball. Rachel catches up with them
and says something to Snail Boy.
Ellie watches. A minute later,
Rachel returns.

Ellie "What did you say to them? Will I get my netball back?"

Rachel "Um, sort of."

Ellie "Sort of? What d'ya mean sort of?"

Rachel "Well, I tried to get them to have another netball showdown."

Ellie "What?"

Rachel "But they said no."

Ellie "Good. I couldn't take losing again for us."

Rachel "So I challenged them to a soccer shoot-out instead."

Ellie "You did what?"

Rachel "It's the only way we've got any hope of getting your ball back."

Ellie "No, it isn't. I'm gonna tell my dad what's happened."

Rachel "Okay. But by the time you do that they'll be long gone, laughing their heads off. And they'll get home and *still* be making fun of us. Imagine if they took the ball to some secret hideaway on a deserted island and gave it magical powers and ..."

Ellie "Dream on! As if."

Rachel "Mmm. Maybe not, but let's do this soccer thing and show them. I said we'd meet at the soccer goals. We all have to take a penalty shot for goal and again, the team with the most goals will win your ball."

Ellie "From netball to soccer. This is just crazy. But let's go and get it over with."

CHAPTER 5

Final Showdown

Ellie and Rachel meet the boys in front of the soccer goal. The boys decide to kick for goals first so Rachel is goalie. Snail Boy lines up his penalty shot and kicks the ball hard. Rachel dives to her left and punches the ball away.

Ellie (shouting) "Unreal! That was amazing. You saved it."

Rachel "I know. How good was that!"

As Snail Boy stamps his foot in frustration, Bulldog Boy prepares to take his shot. He takes a long run up and … *thump!* The ball whizzes over Rachel and the crossbar, missing the goal completely.

Rachel "Yes! No score to the boys.
This is our chance, El. I'll go first. I
know I can get a goal. Then we can
grab your ball and we're outta here!"

Rachel places the netball on the
penalty mound with Snail Boy as
goalie. Rachel takes in a deep breath
and ... *thump!* She kicks the ball
hard along the ground but Snail Boy
stops it with his foot and saves it.

Ellie "Oh no, my turn. We'll lose again, for sure!"

Rachel "Sorry Ellie, but if you miss, we're history. So go on, take your shot."

Ellie (sighing) "Okay, here goes nothing."

Ellie places the ball on the penalty
spot and takes a few steps back. She
runs at the ball and boots it as hard
as she can. The ball flies through the
air at an incredible speed. It zips
past Snail Boy and into the back of
the net. It's a goal!

Rachel "Woo hoo! You got it! You got it!"

Ellie "I know, I know! I got it! I got it!"

The boys toss the netball back at the girls and storm off in a huff.

Rachel "El, you got your ball back. And y'know what this means?"

Ellie "What?"

Rachel "Soccer's your sport. Forget netball, you're a soccer star!"

Ellie "Yeah, I guess I am."

Rachel GIRLZ ROCK! **Netball Lingo** *Ellie*

free pass You get a free pass when the player you're playing against does something wrong.

offside When a player crosses into an area that they are not allowed to be in.

three seconds A penalty against a player who holds the ball for more than three seconds before passing it.

throw in One team gets to throw the ball in from the sideline if the other team makes the ball go out of the court.

toss-up When both players have possession of the ball, it is tossed into the air between them. The one that catches it first gets to pass.

GIRLZ ROCK!
Netball Must-dos

⭐ You must pass the ball or shoot for a goal within three seconds.

⭐ Practise shouting out loudly, to get your team mates' attention.

⭐ Remember to take off all your jewellery before playing so you won't poke or scratch anyone, including yourself!

⭐ Cheer for your team mates, and encourage them if they do something good.

⭐ Practise whenever and wherever you can. Try throwing goals into a bucket in your backyard.

☆ Shake your opponent's hand after the game, even if your team loses.

☆ Bring something warm to wear after the game. Remember, netball's a winter sport!

☆ Make up a team chant to perform with your team members before your game—it will really put you in the mood!

Netball Instant Info

- Australia has won more world championships in netball than any other country.

- The longest match of netball ever played lasted 50 hours. That game was played in South Africa in 2001.

- A netball court is 30.5 metres long and 15.25 metres wide.

- A netball court is divided into three sections.

- Netballs are usually made from leather or rubber.

A netball weighs between 400 and 500 grams.

Each player wears a bib with the initials for their position e.g. "GA" is "Goal Attack". These make the positions clear to the players, spectators and umpires.

Australia is the best netball nation in the world.

Netball is not an Olympic sport but it is hoped it will be in the future.

GIRLZ ROCK!

Think Tank

1 How can you practise shooting goals at home if you don't have a netball ring?

2 What should you do if boys steal your netball?

3 What creatures do the boys in the story remind the girls of?

4 What is a "free pass" (not the kind you use at the movies)?

5 How high do you think the netball ring is—2.4 metres or 1 metre?

6 What is one of the best ways to make sure your netball team wins?

7 Who wears a bib in netball?

8 Which season is netball played in?

Answers

1 You can practise shooting at home by throwing the ball into a bucket.

2 You challenge them to a soccer shoot-out.

3 The boys remind the girls of a bulldog and a snail.

4 A free pass is given to the other player when you do something wrong.

5 A netball hoop is 2.4 metres high.

6 Make up a team chant and recite it before each game—your team is sure to win!

7 All players wear a bib to show what position they are playing.

8 Netball is played in winter.

How did you score?

- If you got 8 answers correct, then maybe you should try out for the Australian netball team.

- If you got 6 or more answers correct, you like netball and probably already play in a team. If you don't, maybe you should try it.

- If you got fewer than 4 answers correct, then maybe you might like to try basketball.

39

Hey Girls!

I hope that you have as much fun reading my story as I have had writing it. I loved reading and writing stories when I was young.

Here are some suggestions that might help you enjoy reading even more than you do now.

At school, why don't you use "Netball Showdown" as a play and you and your friends can be the actors. Get a netball, some netball bibs (make your own if you can't get hold of any) and a ball to use as props. So ... have you decided who is going to be Ellie and who is going to be Rachel? And what about the narrator?

Now act out the story in front of your friends. I'm sure you'll all have a great time!

You also might like to take this story home and get someone in your family to read it with you. Maybe they can take on a part in the story.

Whatever you choose to do, you can have as much fun with reading and writing as a polar bear in a freezer!

And remember, Girlz Rock!

Jacqueline Saena

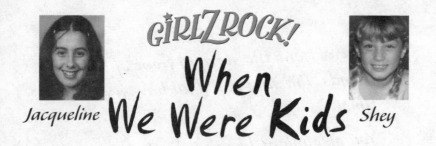

GIRLZ ROCK!
When We Were Kids

Jacqueline · *Shey*

Jacqueline talked to Shey, another *Girlz Rock!* author

Jacqueline "Were you good at netball when you were young?"

Shey "Yep, still am. I'm a champion!"

Jacqueline "Really?"

Shey "Yeah, I'm so good that I played for Australia."

Jacqueline "That's unreal!"

Shey "I was really disappointed, though. We won, but I never got my medal!"

Jacqueline "Why not?"

Shey "Mum woke me up just before they presented me with mine!"